# VANISHED IN CLEVELAND

REBECCA GALLO

# DEAR READER

Not all made men are created equal. Some rule with absolute tyranny, while others take a more diplomatic approach. The characters in *Vanished in Cleveland* represent the best and the worst of the criminal underworld. Some readers might be sensitive to specific scenes in the book involving violence against women (TW: SA/SV) and violence in general. Read with caution.

# ONE

## ALEKSY

THE SIGHT of my enemy on his knees, begging for my help, warms my cold heart.

Massimo Giordano rambles about his daughter, Luciana, but it's hard to focus on what he's saying because his presence distracts me. For years, I've struggled in this city, and Massimo is handing me the perfect opportunity to finally acquire the power I desire.

"Stop," I bark. "And start over. This time, speak clearly. I couldn't understand a goddamn word you said. Don't they speak English in Youngstown?"

His eyes widen before he clears his throat, lifting a hand to straighten his black tie. "Tytus Nowak has my daughter, Lucia."

"And how do you know the Nowaks took her?" There's no doubt Tytus and his dirty band of brothers would kidnap Lucia Giordano and make her a part of their illicit auctions, but I need to be certain Massimo isn't trying to start a war between my family and the Nowaks. I wouldn't put it past a ruthless dago like Massimo Giordano to intentionally stir up bad blood between the two primary Polish mob families in

Cleveland. The families in Youngstown have been trying to make their way west into Cleveland after failing miserably to make a mark in Pittsburgh. Their power in Youngstown is undeniable; nothing happens in that godforsaken city without the approval of the Giordanos. Forming an alliance with them would make me more powerful than the Nowaks, giving me the edge I need to completely control Cleveland.

He holds out a shaky hand, a cell phone clutched in his fingers. "They sent this."

He unlocks the phone and hands it to me, the black screen coming to life. A video is cued up and waiting as soon as I swipe my finger to unlock the phone. I press play and immediately, the sight of Lucia Giordano, bound and bloody, comes into view. My free hand clenches into a fist, almost a reflex. Tytus Nowak is known for his brutality, and the rumors about how he treats the women he sells seem to be true. My blood boils as the video continues. Tytus's brother, Filip, comes into view and Lucia starts to scream. There's no audio but her mouth opens wide and her body shakes until he manages to inject something in her arm. Within minutes, her entire body slumps.

The Nowaks will pay.

"I'll give you anything you want," Massimo says, his voice thick and heavy with emotion.

Anything? The possibilities of what I could ask for are endless but other than power, there's only one thing I desire.

"If I do this, Lucia is mine." She's promised to a son from the Bianchi family, but I can't lose sight of what I want, which means Massimo must break a few promises if he wants his precious *principessa* back.

"Done," he says without hesitation. "Is that all?"

His naivety makes me laugh. As if marrying his daughter would be enough to start a war with the Nowaks. I've been calculating the risks of heading into one of Tytus's auctions. Human cargo is not my preferred currency. Weapons? Illegal gambling? Money laundering? Sign me up. But human trafficking is a line I will not cross.

"Once we're married, I become your underboss."

He scoffs. "That's not happening. Nero will become underboss, not some Polack."

I shrug. "Then Lucia will be sold off to someone who will no doubt ruin her."

"You cannot ask me to take away my son's inheritance. He deserves his place as my underboss. You are already the head of the Zajak family. Isn't an alliance between our two families good enough?"

I set the cell phone on my desk and lean back in my leather chair. "I've been the head of the Zajak family for almost five years because some Irish thug murdered my father. For fifteen years, I've struggled to make my mark, and now, the opportunity to become one of the most powerful men in all Northeast Ohio is staring me right in the face. To answer your question, no, an alliance is not good enough. I want a merger. You retain your role as boss, and I will become your underboss."

I noticed the shift in his expression when I said the word "merger." He knows uniting with the Zajaks will allow him access to Cleveland, something he's tried to gain only to fail.

"Think about it," I murmur as I pick up the phone and watch the video again. She's young, not even twenty-one, and I'm almost certain she's still a virgin, which Tytus will exploit to drive up the price and line his pockets.

"You have a deal," Massimo says.

"Excellent," I purr, extending my hand. "Pleasure doing business with you."

I regret not having my lawyer present to draw up the terms and make this arrangement legally binding, but Massimo is old school, the kind of man who doesn't back out of a handshake deal, the kind of man who believes a man's world is worth more than the price of gold. When he leaves, I call in my brother, Jakub.

"I need you to get me into Tytus Nowak's next auction," I tell him.

"Are you serious?" he asks with a surprised tone.

"Very."

"But those auctions—"

"Aren't the kind of thing we normally do. I'm making an exception."

"Why?"

I roll my eyes. Sometimes Jakub and I are mistaken for twins, but our looks are where the similarity ends. He is an excellent underboss. He manages his capos and soldiers well; they respect him and me. He doesn't take risks, though. He has no desire for more than what we already have, which is plenty. But it's not enough for me.

I don't want to be beholden to anyone.

I don't want to kneel in front of anyone.

I want to own Northeast Ohio.

"I agreed to find Lucia Giordano."

He blinks. "She's been kidnapped?"

I nod. "By the Nowaks." I tap my fingers on the desk before telling him the rest of my deal with Massimo Giordano. "If I uphold my end of the bargain, it will mean some big changes to our family. It will give the Zajak name real power."

"Yes, but uniting with the Giordanos?" He rolls his

head and tugs at the collar of his shirt. "Our men aren't going to like it."

"Too bad," I snap. "I'm going to marry Lucia, and Massimo will make me underboss. They'll either fall in line or find another family to serve."

"Our men are loyal, Aleksy. You know they'll follow you into battle. But don't do anything to betray them."

"Just get me into the auction, Jakub, and leave the rest to me."

# TWO

## LUCIA

I'M A BITCH. A cruel, heartless bitch and I don't care.

"Shut up," I snap to the girls being held in the cell next to mine, but they're too doped up to even notice what's going on around them.

"Have a little sympathy for them," someone mumbles.

I turn my head in the opposite direction, searching for the voice. It's so dark in here, we're all reduced to shapes. "Sympathy? We're all probably going to die. I don't want my last moments on Earth to be spent listening to them moan and cry."

The girl chuckles. "So, what should they do instead? Braid each other's hair?"

I roll my eyes. "I don't know, but I wasn't raised to be weak." A long sigh escapes my lips. "What's your name?"

"Tia."

"I'm Lucia," I tell her. There's more I want to say but a door bangs open and a well-dressed man appears, striding forward with a cocky swagger and a smirk on his lips.

"Good morning, *królewna*," he greets me. "Did you sleep well?"

"About as well as you'd expect considering you kidnapped and drugged me," I snap.

He laughs and from the lecherous glare in his eye, I'm grateful for the barrier between us. "You have a smart mouth."

"Fuck you," I seethe.

He chuckles. "Many women would like that honor. Maybe even you?"

I huff out a laugh. "Don't bet on it. I'd never be desperate enough to sleep with a Polack."

He cups his crotch, squeezing it. "You might think differently if I showed you my cock."

"You could have the biggest dick in the world and I wouldn't give a fuck. When my father and his men find you, you're going to wish you never stepped foot in Mahoning Valley."

He slowly paces in front of my cell, licking his lips as his gaze traces hotly across my body, making my skin crawl. "Taking you was a risk, *królewna*, but you know what they say about men with big cocks, don't you?"

"Tiny brains?"

He comes to a stop and runs a hand along his jaw. "Perhaps you'd like a demonstration?"

"What?" I turn my head and watch as he approaches the cell with the moaning girls. He pulls a key ring from his pocket; it jangles as he searches for the right key before fitting it into the lock. When he enters the cell, my stomach churns. "Stop. Please."

His gaze slides over to me briefly before he strides forward and selects a girl, fisting his hand through her hair and dragging her to her knees. She whimpers, but whatever drugs she's been given make her compliant.

"Open your mouth," he pants as he unbuckles his pants.

My father taught me to be smart, and right now, I feel foolish. There was nothing I could have done to prevent the situation I'm in, but I regret my cruelty toward the other girls. I should have been patient and sympathetic. They're innocent too, and now, one is being punished for my stubbornness.

"What do you think, *królewna?* Is my cock big enough for you?"

"Stop," I beg with a shaky breath as I watch him smear the tip of his cock along the girl's lips. Bile rises in my throat and burns as I vomit, forcing the man to laugh. I keep my eyes clenched shut, unable to watch the horrific act but the sounds are unescapable, despite my efforts to cover my ears.

I'm no stranger to the brutal underworld of the Mahoning Valley but my father, my brothers, their soldiers . . . would never resort to this level of depravity.

Hot tears stream down my cheeks as his grunts grow louder and louder until a feral growl fills the air. My body convulses with sobs.

"Who are you," I whimper.

"A man even the devil is afraid of."

My eyes open slowly, watching him zip up and button his pants. The girl is still on her knees, completely unaware of what she's endured. Guilt splits my heart in two. Maybe if I kept my mouth shut, he wouldn't have been provoked.

When he leaves, a collective sigh escapes all our lips.

"Now you know why I told you to have some sympathy," Tia says. The cold tone of her voice forces a sob to escape my lips.

"I'm sorry," I cry. "I'm so sorry."

"Accept your fate, sister," she tells me with the same chilly tone.

"Listen, I'm sorry for being a bitch." The bitterness of

my words is unexpected until I realize my guilt has morphed into anger. "But my father is a powerful man. He's probably working on a plan to rescue me right now."

"Who are you trying to convince? Me or yourself?"

"He's coming," I repeat, knowing it's me who needs persuading.

My father is strong and intimidating. I've seen him make men cry, force them to their knees and beg for mercy, but something about this situation feels different. Desperate. Hopeless. I must believe he's going to save me, otherwise I'll crumble like the girls in the next cell.

This is not my fate, I repeat silently—until the door opens again and someone comes for me.

# THREE

## ALEKSY

EVERYONE KNOWS Cleveland belongs to the Nowaks, the most notorious Polish mafia family, but tonight, I'm playing in their territory. If I want to move up in the world, I need to stick close to my enemies.

When I arrive at Tytus Nowak's sprawling estate, no one bats an eye at my appearance. They're too stupid to even realize who I am because every time I've tried to make a name for myself, Tytus is there to remind me of my place.

The mansion is extensive with a who's who of Northeast Ohio's criminal underworld. Italian. Irish. Polish. Mexican. They're all here mixing and mingling for one nefarious purpose.

The auction.

The disgusting thing about my enemy is his preferred method of criminal activity.

Human trafficking.

Maybe that's why I'm still a little fish in a big pond. My family, the Zajaks, runs the unions and an underground gambling ring. We're good at hiding money. We're even better at rigging elections. I prefer my money not covered in blood, so I do my best to keep my family away from drugs and guns. They're last resorts.

"Aleksy." The sound of Tytus's voice stops me. I turn to face him and bow my head in deference. "What are you doing here?"

I plaster on a cool smile. "I thought I'd diversify my portfolio."

He laughs. "So, the Zajaks are interested in this sort of cargo?"

"Tempted. It's why I'm here tonight."

His eyes narrow and he hums as if deciding whether I'm telling the truth. I'm not. Every word out of my mouth is a lie. There's only one reason I'm here: Lucia Giordano.

"Enjoy your evening, then," he says, raising the glass in his hand in silent toast.

"Before you go, I heard a rumor that Lucia Giordano will be on the auction block tonight. Is that true?"

Any trace of hospitality disappears from his expression. "Where did you hear that?"

*From her father.* "Our community isn't very big, Tytus. One of my men told me. He heard it on the streets."

He inhales deeply and then exhales, his mouth turned down into a frown. "If Lucia Giordano interests you, then you'll need to make your way to the basement."

"What's in the basement?"

"My secondary auction. I've accumulated a collection of rare beauties."

"Thank you for the invitation. That might be of more interest to me than a truckload of children."

"A word of advice, Aleksy? Proceed with caution. I don't know how you found your way here tonight, but if you think this is the place for you, I'll allow you to stay."

My jaw clenches. This is how he always acts toward

me. Superior. Smug. His family might be more powerful than mine but his days ruling Cleveland are numbered. This is the first step toward taking over Northeast Ohio.

"You'll need this to get in," he says, handing me a black key card before disappearing into the crowd.

The card feels heavy in my hand. I'm about to spend an obscene amount of money to get what I want.

I don't have to worry about where to find the basement. All I have to do is follow the men dressed in impeccably tailored suits who ooze greed and lechery. At the bottom of a flight of stairs is a door with a bodyguard standing sentry. He stops us, and each of us must swipe the key card across the electronic lock, no doubt to keep track of who enters.

Nerves unexpectedly spring to life inside my belly when it's my turn. This could be a set up. Massimo Giordano was in my office a week ago begging me to help return his daughter, but I wouldn't put it past him to use Lucia as bait. He's tried and failed for years to gain territory in Cleveland.

When the light on the electronic pad flashes from red to green, a sigh escapes my lips. The guard opens the door and admits me into the space. Tytus's basement is a full-blown nightclub complete with walls painted a rich midnight blue, and thumping music heavy on bass. There's a platform in the center of the space with a spotlight shining down on it. No doubt this is where the auction will take place.

Women dressed in scraps travel through the room carrying trays of champagne, stopping to flutter their lashes at men who salivate as they pick up a glass.

It's a repulsive show and the moment I've acquired Lucia, I'll be gone.

I grab a glass off a tray as a woman passes by me. She slides her cat-like gaze over to me but when she realizes I'm not in the mood for anything she might have to offer, she keeps walking.

A few faces in the crowd are familiar as I walk around, sipping the champagne. It's cold and crisp, the perfect antidote for my nerves. Some of the men sneer as I pass by them, and some glance at me with curious eyes. They know I'm at as out of place as I feel.

The music ends and the voices in the room quiet as Tytus makes his way through the crowd to the platform.

"Good evening, gentlemen," he announces. "Tonight's auction will begin shortly so find a seat and open your wallets. We've got some very special items tonight."

There's a rush toward the seats placed around the makeshift stage. I find an empty leather club chair in the front row toward a dark corner, the perfect place to watch, learn, and ultimately, win.

"All bidding will be conducted electronically. Please click on the link sent to your phone. It will open our system. All bidders must be registered," he continues to explain.

I look around at everyone pulling out their phones and follow, taking my phone out from a pocket inside my jacket. True to his word, there's a text from an unknown number. The message is simply a link which I click. Once the bidding system pops up on my phone, I enter the information required until I get confirmation of my successful registration. This is quite a sophisticated set-up for such a sinister scheme.

When the auction officially begins, a man in a tuxedo leads a young girl on stage, parading her around for everyone to see. From the vacant expression in the girl's eyes, she seems drugged. She stumbles a few times and then giggles incoherently. After a few minutes, she's lead away, and another girl is brought onto the stage. This continues for a while. I expect to recognize some of the girls, but none are familiar.

"And now for what you've all been waiting for," Tytus announces. "You know me, I like to save the best for last."

The man in the tuxedo brings out three girls. They're chained to each other, linked by long silver chains attached to cuffs wrapped around their wrists.

Lucia is in the middle. Her eye is bruised, and her lip is split, but she doesn't have the same vacant expression as the others. The two girls flanking her seem to have accepted tonight's outcome; she appears ready to fight. I catch her tugging at the restraints with barely noticeable movements. She's smart but if she doesn't stop, Tytus and his men will notice and punish her.

She's wearing a skimpy black dress barely covering her curves. The slinky fabric hugs her body, leaving nothing to the imagination. The two girls chained to her are dressed similarly in dresses designed to reveal as much as possible. Though the other girls look familiar, I don't know who they are. Knowing Tytus, they probably also belong to prominent families. Hopefully, someone comes to rescue them.

I stand and circle the stage with the other men who are prowling around like rabid dogs. They salivate as they run their fat, greasy hands over the girls, letting them wander over every inch of bare skin. Two of the girls stand coldly beside Lucia, who turns green as one man slides his hand up her thigh.

*Don't you dare. She's mine.*

Before I have the chance to rip off the man's arm, Tytus steps onto the stage in front of the girls and lifts his foot, pressing it against the man's forehead. "Look but don't touch," he seethes as he forces the man away from the stage with the sole of his shoe.

"The bidding for these rare and precious jewels will start at one million," he announces.

"Five million for the one in the middle," I call out.

His gaze lands on me and his cruelty is replaced with a calculating grin. "Someone's an eager beaver."

"I know what I want," I reply firmly. "And I can pay cash."

"Sold," he says without even offering anyone else the opportunity to bid on Lucia.

So predictable. Cash is always king.

"I want her now," I demand.

"The night isn't over."

"It is for me. Do as I say, or I'll take my business and my money elsewhere."

Tytus rolls his eyes and then gestures to a set of guards standing nearby. "Uncuff her," he instructs them. "I want my money before I hand her over."

"Of course. It's in my car."

His eyes widen. "You left five million dollars in cash inside your car? Christ, Aleksy. You really are a stupid Polack."

"Shut the fuck up and follow me. Bring the girl." I turn on my heel and make my way through the crowd to the door before heading up the stairs. I glance behind me a few times to keep an eye on Lucia. She seems relieved to be free, but her mouth is a hard line of anger.

There's a valet stand in front of the house and I slide my ticket to the attendant. "I'm leaving."

While we wait, I shrug out of my jacket and approach Lucia to place it across her bare shoulders.

"Such a gentleman," Tytus teases.

"It's freezing and she's wearing scraps," I tell him through clenched teeth.

"What's your point?" He rolls his eyes and snickers.

"I'm paying five million dollars for her. I don't want her to die from hypothermia. Unless you're offering a money-back guarantee."

"All sales are final."

When the attendant arrives with my car, I reach for Lucia's hand but Tytus pulls her back. "Money first."

"Fine." Each step toward the car is deliberate. I can't reveal my hand too soon. It would ruin everything.

I open the passenger door and lean inside, grabbing the briefcase from the back seat. It's heavy in my hand as I grip the handle and back away, straightening myself before glancing back at Tytus, whose eyes glitter with greed.

He uncuffs Lucia and pushes her toward me. "Get my money," he snarls.

She skitters across the pavement and reaches for the case in my hand. "Get in the car," I tell her. When she's settled in the passenger seat, I walk back to Tytus and hand him the briefcase.

He seems pleased with the weight of the case. "Pleasure doing business with you," he sneers.

"It's been a blast."

# FOUR

## LUCIA

"WE HAVE TO GO BACK." I twist in my seat and watch Tytus Nowak's estate slowly fade into the darkness of the night.

"No way in hell," Aleksy says.

"But the other girls—"

"Are probably going to die." He sighs and steers the car onto a dead-end street. "Listen, we need to get the fuck away from this place because as soon as that asshole opens the briefcase, there's going to be a very big explosion. I'm sorry for what's about to happen to them but getting you out of there was my priority."

A crushing weight settles on my chest. "Oh, God," I choke out. "How could you do this to them? They're innocent!"

*Tia is innocent.* We didn't know each other for long but I knew her name, knew she was a person. Her life matters as much as mine.

He puts the car into gear and backs up. "It doesn't matter whether they're innocent or not. Tytus took something that didn't belong to him, and he needs to pay."

"And that means murdering innocent girls too?"

His hands flex over the steering wheel, gripping it tight. This is the first time I've met Aleksy Zajak, though I've heard his name mentioned often in my house. He's not at all what I expected. Instead of someone big and brutal, he looks more like a lawyer or a banker. His suit is tailored and probably custom. His sandy brown hair with touches of gray is smoothed back, and his beard is meticulously groomed.

"I'm sorry they might become collateral damage, truly, but I did what your father asked me to do."

"My father sent you?"

"Even a desperate man will turn to his enemy for help."

"I don't believe you," I snap because I know my father. He runs Mahoning Valley. He's a proud Italian man and rules over his family with an iron fist. He'd never let any of the Polish families step foot in his territory without a fight. "Take me home right now."

"That's not going to happen, principessa. You're not safe there."

"My father will make sure I'm safe."

"Just like he kept you safe from the Nowaks?" He shakes his head as he navigates the car toward the highway. "It's time you trust me, Lucia. I'm your fiancé now. Keeping you safe is my number one priority."

"My father would never agree to a marriage between our families."

He glances toward me, his eyebrows raised. "I'm beginning to think you don't know your father very well. Marrying you was a part of the price your father paid for my help, although your beauty alone makes it seem more like a reward."

My stomach churns and my lip curls into a snarl. "You

can keep your eyes to yourself, Polack. My hand in marriage is the only thing you'll get from me."

The hard lines of his face soften, and he sighs. "I'm sorry the Nowaks hurt you. Even though is seems like they were raised by wolves, they weren't. They had a mother, and she was lovely. Made delicious *kolaczki.*"

"Don't do that," I mutter.

"Do what?"

"Humanize them. You weren't there. You didn't see what he did." A violent shudder rips through me imagining what Tytus did to the girl in the cell next to mine.

We travel up the highway in silence. I'm not familiar with the area but there are signs pointing me home. We pass each one. Every mile Aleksy drives seems like a million. I sigh, hug his jacket tighter and lean my head against the window of the car. The clean scent of his cologne hits my nose. It's a heavenly smell and I find comfort in it.

"I need to talk to my father," I murmur as my eyelids flutter with heaviness. This is the first time in days I've felt relaxed and right now, I want to sleep, but not without answers.

"I'll arrange it," he responds tersely.

"Where do you live?"

"Bratenhal."

"I don't know where that is."

His laugh is soft, providing another moment of comfort. Maybe he's not as bad as my father says. "I'm not surprised. Your father probably never let you out of his sight."

"He let me go to college and live on campus."

"Well, you won't be going back. Now that you're mine, I won't let go of you so easily."

I want to argue with him about going back to college, but my exhaustion clouds my thoughts. It's a battle for another day. But when he calls me his, when he says I belong to him? I know how I should feel. He should scare me. I know what kind of man he is, the kind of destruction he can cause, but I can't bring myself to feel that way. Maybe it's the shock of being rescued from a hellish situation and tomorrow, when I wake up, everything will feel differently.

Except, when he glances over at me while we're driving, there's something in his eye. His face is hard and impassive, but his gaze betrays him.

"My house is on the lake. It has a private beach. You'll like it."

I wrinkle my nose. "Lake Erie is so gross. My father has a beach house in Florida. Maybe you should just send me there."

He chuckles and mumbles something in Polish, but I don't quite hear it because my eyes close and my body melts into the seat.

"We're home." The sound of Aleksy's whisper shakes me from my nap. When I start to move, he places a gentle hand on my shoulder. "I've got you. Just put your arms around my neck and I'll do all the hard work."

My arms feel like lead as I slide them up his chest and link them around his neck. His hands are warm against my cold, bare skin as he shifts me out of the passenger seat and into his embrace. I keep my eyes closed, refusing to open them. This seems to be a dream and when I wake up, I don't want to realize I'm still trapped in a nightmare.

"Thank you," I tell him with a sigh, pressing my cheek against his warm chest.

"For what?"

"Saving me."

"Don't thank me yet, *królewna*. I'm not the knight in shining armor you think I am."

My eyes flutter open and it's like seeing Aleksy for the first time. His brutal beauty is breathtaking. From a distance he's handsome, but up close, his scars are visible. There's one slashing through his eyebrow and another on his chin. His nose is slightly crooked. He's been through battle, through wars. He stepped into enemy territory for me tonight.

"No, you're not," I murmur. "You're something else entirely."

"What? What am I?"

"*Sei un re*. You're a king."

# FIVE
## ALEKSY

IN THE MORNING, Lucia will regret everything, but for now, I'm going to enjoy having an angel in my arms.

My reaction to seeing her for the first time was unexpected. She took my breath away. All it took was a singular moment to realize I'd walk through fire for this woman.

She's mine now. I'll protect her with every fiber of my being, even if it means protecting her from me.

I carry her through the house to the master bedroom and set her gently on the bed. She dozed in the car but now, her exhaustion is too much and she's fast asleep. When she slips out of my arms and onto the mattress, she rolls to her side, tugging my jacket tighter across her body. I reach for a blanket folded across the end of the bed and pull it up to cover her bare legs.

I need to call a doctor. She needs to be examined, even if her wounds are superficial. There's no telling what Tytus and his men did to her, or what kind of drugs they put into her system.

My phone buzzes in my pocket. I pull it out and read

the news—a blast in Medina at the estate of Tytus Nowak. No word on survivors yet.

I shove my phone back into my pocket and glance up at Lucia one last time before leaving. My work tonight isn't over.

As I make my way down to my office, my brother Jakub appears from the shadows. "Did you see the news?"

"Yes. It's a tragedy."

He follows me into my office, which used to belong to my father. In fact, much of what I have today was his. My role as the head of the Zajak family. My home on prestigious Lake Shore Drive. My membership to the ultra-exclusive Shore Club. His constant shadow hangs over my life.

But this deal with the Giordanos is mine. Taking out the Nowaks is a victory I can claim as my own.

And soon, Lucia will also belong to me.

"What's the plan, Aleksy?" Jakub sounds worried, and when I finally look up him, I see the glisten of sweat along his brow.

"Are you nervous, brother?"

"Taking this kind of risk isn't like you," he says.

I blink. "I've always been upfront about my desire to make the Zajak family powerful. Aren't you sick and tired of being second-best, Jakub? Don't you want to run this town?"

"Of course I want that, but blowing up the Nowak estate? Killing Tytus and whoever else was there tonight? That's a lot of blood on your hands. How can you be certain Massimo Giordano isn't setting you up?"

"I'm not," I tell him honestly. "But we know the Nowaks and what they're into. They had Lucia. I was there tonight, in his basement, taking part in one of those disgusting auctions. He asked me to get her out and I did. I only regret not getting the others."

I place my hands flat on my desk and stare at them. Jakub is right. There is a lot of blood on my hands tonight. My father instilled in us the desire to exact retribution with minimal collateral damage. He never wanted the life we live to spill onto the streets.

"This deal better be worth the shit we're going to get," Jakub says before standing. "Get some sleep, brother. We need to look at this situation with fresh eyes."

When he leaves, I make my way over to the bar near the window and pour myself a shot of vodka. It stings as I swallow, and burns in my blood.

Tonight rattled my confidence, and as I make my way through the house to my bedroom, I wonder if I made the right decision. I stop just outside the master bedroom, opening the door a crack. Lucia is still asleep, just as I left her. What will she think in the morning once she realizes the gravity of the situation?

If I'm lucky she'll stay, but something tells me I'll be fighting to keep her.

My phone buzzes again, notifying me of a text message. It's from Massimo.

**Massimo: Is Lucia safe?**

**Me: Yes.**

**Massimo: Is she hurt?**

**Me: Come by tomorrow and see for yourself. I'll arrange for a doctor if necessary.**

**Massimo: I saw the news.**

**Me: I did what needed to be done. We can discuss it tomorrow.**

**Massimo: Thank you.**

My own exhaustion creeps into my bones. I empty my pockets, placing the items on top of a nearby dresser before undressing. My clothes fall to the floor in a heap; they can wait until tomorrow to be picked up. Right now, I want to lay down and try to not let doubt creep into my thoughts. Jakub never questions me, but seeing him sweating and nervous shook me. If I didn't make the right choice, if I walked into a trip, then I risked the Zajak family, my men, their families—everything my father built when he arrived in this country as a poor immigrant escaping post-World War II Poland. I can't let any of them down.

But when I close my eyes, Lucia's face is all I see.

I'd seen her before. Massimo paraded her in front of his army of goombahs the moment she turned eighteen, and promised her to the Bianchi family and their pathetic son, Julian. Even from a distance, her beauty was obvious, but two things prevented me from taking any interest. One is her age. The considerable age gap between us seems almost impossible. The second is of course the bad blood between our families. As much as I respect her father's power, we're still considered enemies, fighting for a bigger piece of the pie. There wasn't a reason for me to sniff around her because a few years ago, I wasn't interested in joining forces with the Giordanos.

I push any more thoughts of Lucia out of my mind and spend the next few hours fighting a restless sleep until I hear the door across the hall open. I sit up in bed as if struck by a bolt of lightning and wait, listening to the sound of her footsteps as she walks up and down the hall.

I'm not surprised when she eventually pushes the door to my bedroom open. "I want to go home," she declares with a pout.

She's abandoned my jacket and stands in the doorway

still dressed in the skimpy black dress the Nowaks forced her to wear. There are more bruises covering her creamy porcelain skin. I didn't see them last night, but I was too distracted to notice more than the obvious.

"I see you've abandoned any feelings of gratitude you might have felt last night," I joke as I slip out of bed and reach for a pair of sweatpants before shuffling across the room toward her. "How are you feeling?"

She watches me with a careful eye but the moment I raise a hand, her guard is up. "Don't touch me."

"Being stubborn won't get you anywhere. Let me look, *królewna*; I won't hurt you.

"Fine," she answers as I run gentle fingers over her arms, inspecting a few black-and-blue marks before grasping her chin between my thumb and forefinger. After a few tense minutes, I release my grip and decide a doctor isn't necessary. "I want to go back to my own home."

"This is your home now," I tell her firmly.

"No, it's not," she says with a bit of a pout.

"Your father will be here soon enough. You can argue with him if you wish, but I suspect you won't get your way. A deal's a deal."

"So, you're going to steal my life from me? You're just like the Nowaks."

"I am nothing like them," I growl. "You'll learn that soon enough."

"And you should learn I don't like being a pawn in these sick games you play."

"The deal I made to save you from the Nowaks isn't part of some game, Lucia. I've paid my dues in this world and it's time I rise to finally claim what's mine."

"Why do I have to be a part of that? You rescued me, now let me go."

Having her so close is tempting. I remind myself of what she's been through. Who knows what the Nowaks did to her or what she had to witness? There's no need to cause more harm, not when I want her to trust me to keep her safe. "I don't think I can do that."

The way she looks up at me with her big jade green eyes is so fucking innocent. How could she not know what she's doing right now? How could she not know how beautiful she is? Like Helen of Troy. And last night, I'm certain I started a war.

"Why not?"

"Isn't it obvious?"

"Not to me." Her voice is barely a whisper. Tension crackles between us.

I know what I should do. Step away. Leave her alone. She's vulnerable and anything I might do would take advantage of an impossible situation.

I am better than this. But when I decide to strike, to slip my hand over the curve of her waist, she doesn't shy away. There's no push back.

"Tell me to stop and I will," I tell her. "Tell me not to touch you. Tell me you've just been through hell and back and need time to process. Fuck, *królewna*, give me some excuse to back away."

"I'm still a virgin." A blush spreads across her cheeks, painting them a velvety pink.

"Do you really think that will stop me?" By now, my cock is aching, and I've done nothing to hide my hardness from her.

"No, but I thought you should know."

Voices from the front of the house filter up to my bedroom. One voice stands out above the rest. Massimo.

The sound is like ice cold water, forcing me to realize that having sex with Lucia right now would have been a mistake.

"Your father is here," I state before pushing away.

"He can't see me like this."

There's no hesitation when I reach up and brush my fingers along the ugly bruise on her face. "I can find you something to wear but this will be harder to conceal."

I turn away, ready to head into the closet, but Lucia reaches for my hand and pulls me back. She pops up onto her tiptoes, wraps an arm around my neck and presses her lips against mine. Her lips are warm and inviting but with an innocent hesitation, as if she's unsure I'll return the kiss.

I give her my answer by swiftly backing her against the wall, pressing my body against her. I knock her arm away and take charge, cupping her face with my hands, teasing her lips apart with my tongue. I devour every ounce of her sweetness until her hands press against my chest and she gently pushes me back.

"What was that for," I breathe out.

"A thank you," she murmurs. "For saving me last night."

I step into her space again, ready for more but she slides away. "We shouldn't make him wait," she whispers, her gaze averted. There's a fresh bloom of pink on her cheeks, as if she's embarrassed to have kissed me.

"You're right, but next time *królewna*, nothing will stop me from taking what I want."

# SIX

## LUCIA

I'M GETTING in over my head and when Aleksy leaves to meet with my father, I retreat to the bedroom where I slept last night, hoping to find some clarity.

I need to focus on the bigger issue; my life is not my own. It's been this way since I was born. I've lived in a gilded cage, allowed only small moments of freedom, and now, the rest of my life has been negotiated.

I'm grateful to Aleksy and my father for working together to save me from the hell of being sold to the highest bidder at the Nowak's auction, but what my father did isn't much different.

At least this devil I know, but I can't let a handsome face distract me. My attraction to Aleksy is based on adrenaline and nothing more. Once the dust from last night settles, I'm positive the attraction between us will fizzle out.

I speed through getting cleaned up, using whatever is available in the bathroom, and dress in the clothes Aleksy found for me. I wish I could spend more time showering off the grime, but my father and I need to talk. The T-shirt and sweatpants are too big, but they'll suffice. They hide most of the bruises.

"You said she wasn't hurt," my father barks the moment I enter Aleksy's office. He bursts up from his chair and rushes toward me.

"I said she didn't need a doctor," Aleksy says with a cool tone. "She's hurt but it's nothing serious. She'll heal."

I scowl at them both. "Yes, *she'll* heal." I give my father a tight smile and kiss his cheek. "Dad, I'm fine, but we need to talk about the deal you made with Aleksy."

"I did what I had to do," he asserts.

"You freed me from one prison only to lock me in another."

My father rolls his eyes. "Don't be so dramatic, Lucia."

"I'm being dramatic? You're forcing me into an arranged marriage. You're giving away Nero's birthright." Hot tears sting my eyes as I think about the last week. "You don't know what it's like to feel completely helpless. I couldn't fight back like you taught me, and when I tried to be strong and stubborn, do you know what happened? Tytus Nowak punished me. He forced me to watch as he . . . as he . . ." I choke on the rest of the words. I can't say them. I can't tell them what I saw, what I endured, because I don't want to relive it.

Tears stream down my cheeks, blurring my vision. A strong arm wraps around me, tugging me until a familiar clean scent hits my nose.

"You have a choice, *królewna*," Aleksy says. "You don't want to marry me? Fine. I promise not to be too insulted, but you need to hear what your father has to say."

"You're not safe, Lucia," my father tells me, a slight tremor to his voice. "There might have been an explosion last night at the Nowak's estate, but Tytus and his brother

Filip weren't among the dead. They've disappeared, and until we can track them down, you're in danger."

"So, this really is a prison." I nearly choke on the bitterness of my words. "I can't leave this house, can I?"

"No, you can't," Aleksy answers. "It's not ideal but this is the only place you're protected."

"Protected? What makes this place so different from my home in Canfield. I was supposed to be safe there but look what happened. The Nowaks took me from my father's home!"

Aleksy turns me, his hands firm on my shoulders, and lowers himself until we're practically eye to eye. His eyes are icy blue. I never noticed until now. "Look at me," he demands. "You are mine. You belong to me, and I will protect you. I promise you, *królewna*. You are safe with me."

No, I'm not, and we both know it, but neither of us says it out loud. He'll protect me from the Nowaks and any other threat, but when it comes to guarding myself from him? I'm helpless.

"I'm scared," I whisper.

"I know." *Me too*, Aleksy seems to say silently with his expression.

"What if he finds me again?" *What if you hurt me?*

"He won't." *I won't.* "I promise."

"Promises are meant to be broken." I pull away from him and glance back at my father. "I'll stay here until the Nowaks are found, but once this is over, I won't allow my life to be used as some bargaining chip."

I remember Aleksy telling me last night that his house had a private beach, so when I leave his office, that's where I head. After a few wrong turns, I finally make it outside. It's cold and overcast, typical springtime Ohio weather. I head toward a small deck facing the lake and settle into an

Adirondack chair. The wind picks up and even though I start to shiver, I don't move. It's peaceful listening to the waves lapping along the rocky shoreline.

"Planning on swimming to Canada?" Aleksy places a blanket around my shoulders before occupying the seat next to mine.

"Do you know that Virginia Woolf committed suicide by filling the pockets of her dress with rocks and walking into a river?"

"Are you trying to tell me you'd rather die than stay here?"

"I'm simply sharing my thoughts with you."

"As much as I'd love to sit out here with you and contemplate life and death, it's not safe for you out here."

I laugh, though there's nothing funny about the situation. "God, I can't even go outside! I really am trapped."

I shrug off the blanket and stand but stumble over the too-big clothing. Aleksy springs into action, grabbing me before I topple to the sand. He spins me in his arms and holds me tight. His body is warm against mine. I hate the way he already feels so comfortable, how his touch and presence calm me.

He sighs and places a finger under my chin, tilting my face until he's staring down at me. "Just agree to marry me, *królewna*. It will make life easier."

"Why do you keep calling me that? The Nowaks called me that, too. What does it mean?"

"Princess," he says with a grin. "The daughter of a king. And isn't that what you are?"

"The daughter of a king? No. My father is a dictator."

"You can't blame a man for wanting to keep his most prized possessions safe." His hands glide down my back and settle on my waist before disappearing beneath the fabric of the T-shirt I'm wearing. His hands scorch my skin as they brush against me. "I think you were made for more, Lucia. Soon, we will be calling you *królowa*. Queen."

The heat from his body comes off him in waves as he dips his head, our faces inching closer and closer until his breath tickles my skin. "I think that's a more fitting word, don't you?" His voice is soft and sultry, like velvet gliding along my skin.

"Why are you doing this to me?" I ask, inhaling a shaky breath.

"I'm not doing anything to you, Lucia."

"You're forcing me into a marriage I don't want."

Under my shirt, his hands skim my ribs, brushing under my breasts. I suck in a breath, holding it until his touch fades away. "But you want me, don't you?" He spins me until my back is pressed against his front. His hard cock presses against my ass. "Can you feel me, Lucia? You act like marrying me is nothing more than a business transaction but it's not."

"How can it be anything but that?" I break free of his hold and spin to face him. "You don't know me, Aleksy. You call me pretty names, you touch me tenderly, but none of that makes a marriage. You asked for my hand as a part of a negotiation."

"Then teach me, Lucia. Teach me to be a man worthy of you."

"Set me free. If you want to be worthy, let me go. Let me live my own life on my terms."

# SEVEN

## ALEKSY

"YOU KNOW I can't do that." Whatever hope remained inside her seems gone now. Her head drops and she lets out a shaky breath. "But you're right. I don't know you. I'm acting on instinct, but you have to give me the chance to learn."

She squints at me in the sunlight. Her dark hair whips around her face and I notice a few freckles along the bridge of her nose. Her natural beauty is such a fucking turn-on, but apart from her looks, I have no idea who she is as a person.

"I'll consider it," she finally says. "Is my father still here?"

"Yes, we still have some matters to discuss."

"You mean your position as underboss?"

Her perceptiveness makes me smile. "Nothing gets past you."

"My brother will never let that happen."

"Nero doesn't have a choice."

A harsh laugh escapes her lips. "Then you've never met my brother. My father is quite the authoritarian, but Nero is worse. He's ruthless. His form of justice is swift and merciless. Nero doesn't care who you are; if you cross the Giordanos, you're done."

"Is that supposed to scare me?"

"He scares me," she admits. "Maybe he'll kill you, then I don't have to marry you."

"Getting rid of me won't be that easy." I hold out my hand, hoping she'll take it. It doesn't surprise me when she glances at it but chooses to walk past me and up the path back to the house.

She stops when she sees her father waiting on the patio.

"Did you talk some sense into her?" He barks out the question and I notice Lucia's shoulder tense.

"We haven't decided anything," I answer.

"You won't become underboss if she doesn't agree to marry you."

It's almost as if he's drawing a line in the sand, forcing his daughter to make a decision she's uncomfortable making, and jeopardizing any trust she may have in me.

"You came to me and asked me to help get her back. I lived up to my end of the bargain," I remind him through clenched teeth.

"My men won't accept you, you stupid son of a bitch!" He glances over to Lucia and points to me. "Maybe you shouldn't marry him. He seems like a worthless Polack to me."

"Dad, please," she murmurs.

He takes a step toward me, a cocky smile on his lips. "Let me give you a piece of advice, *son.* Any position in the Giordanos is *earned.* I don't fucking care who you are or what family you run. You earn our loyalty and trust before you go around demanding to be my underboss."

Underestimating me is a mistake. Massimo thinks he

can use Lucia to manipulate me into doing his dirty work, into falling in line like a good little soldier. That's not me. That's not the kind of man my father raised, and it's certainly not the leader I've been since I took over the Zajaks.

"When did you know the Nowaks were targeting you, Massimo?" I didn't understand why he came to me for help until now, until he tried to deny me what he promised. "Before or after you sent me to start a war with them?"

He laughs off my questions. "I don't know what the fuck you're talking about."

My gaze narrows. "Yes, you do. If Tytus and his brother Filip are still alive, they're going to come not only for you but they're coming for me and for Lucia. You want me to fight a war without an army?"

"Is this true?" We both turn to face Lucia, whose green eyes are wide with expectation. "You promised to keep me safe."

"I am keeping you safe," he snaps. "I'm trying to keep you the fuck away from Youngstown because I don't know who I can trust! Someone is working with the Nowaks, and I don't know who. Until I figure out who it is, you need to stay here."

"Then make me your goddamn underboss!" Lucia startles at the tone of my voice and immediately, I back away and breathe in deeply. "My army isn't nearly as big as yours. I need more men."

"I'll talk to Nero tonight."

"Tell me where and I'll be there," I demand.

"No, you stay here and keep Lucia safe. I don't want her left alone." He walks across the patio and grabs one of her hands. "I know you think I'm being cruel forcing you into an arranged marriage, taking away what little freedom you were given, but trust me, this is for the best. I came to Aleksy for help for a reason. In a world full of devils and demons, he still has a soul and maybe even a heart."

He lifts her hand to his lips and places a kiss on the back of it before he turns to me, nods, and says, "I can see myself out."

"We need to get inside," I remind Lucia once her father is gone. "It's not safe out here."

She gravitates toward me. I'm not sure she even realizes it until she's next to me. I want to touch her. Fuck, I want to kiss her then strip her bare and feast on her virgin pussy.

"I'll marry you." Her words are unexpected.

"What made you change your mind, *królewna?*" I can't help myself. I lift my hand, grasp a loose strand of her dark hair between my fingers and tuck it behind her ear.

"I was born and raised to be a perfect mafia princess. I know my life will never truly be my own. I don't have control over much, especially who I'm supposed to marry. Technically, I was already promised to Julian Bianchi so how can I be angry over my father breaking one promise while making another? Especially if agreeing to your terms means I am safe from the Nowaks. So, if I refuse to marry you, he's going to force me into marrying someone else."

"Are you saying you're choosing me, *królewna?*"

A pink flush creeps up her neck and colors her pale cheeks. "If I must marry someone, then I'd rather it be you than anyone else. My father is right. You might be one of a dozen devils running around this town, but you still have your soul. You could have been cruel to me like the Nowaks but instead, you've taken care of me."

"*Sprawiasz, że chcę być lepszym człowiekiem,*" I tell her in Polish.

"What does that mean?"

"I'll tell you on the day we get married." I reach up and cup her face with my hands, brushing my thumbs along her cheeks. "You look exhausted. Go and rest for a while."

She nods before retreating inside the house. I slip my cell phone from my pocket and send Jakub a text telling him we need to meet. He needs to know trouble is coming for us.

# EIGHT

## LUCIA

I'M BACK in the cell, wearing the too tight black dress that barely covers me.

*Oh no.* How did I get here? My wrists are cuffed to a table and even though I struggle against the restraints, my movement is limited.

I'm trapped.

"Help," I call out though no one else is with me. Tia isn't in the cell next to mine and the other girls are gone too. "Please, help!"

Anxiety and fear creep into my chest and settle with a heaviness. This is not happening again.

The door opens, revealing a shadowed figure. "*Królewna.*"

"No," I cry. "Please don't hurt me."

"*Królewna,*" he says again before stepping forward.

Hot tears stream down my cheeks as I squeeze my eyes shut. This is a nightmare; it has to be. This isn't real. Aleksy came for me. He saved me.

"Lucia."

My eyes pop open at the sound of my name. "Aleksy?"

He's there, sitting on the edge of the bed with his hands on my shoulders. "You were having a nightmare."

"The Nowaks," I murmur.

"They're never going to hurt you again," he assures me. He leans forward and brushes his hand across my forehead. The gesture is sweet and tender, something my mother used to do when I was younger.

"How long was I asleep?"

"A few hours," he says. The soft sweeping motion of his hand against my skin and the gentle smile on his lips soothe away the leftover demons from my nightmare. "I heard you crying out, so I came to check on you."

"I'm sorry."

"You don't have to apologize for what they did to you or for how you feel about it."

I reach up and grasp his hand, pulling it from my face. I lace my fingers through his and squeeze. "What makes you different from the rest of them?"

"I'm not." The weight of his honesty hangs in the air between us. "I'm as cruel and brutal as your father or Tytus."

"Not to me."

"Would you prefer I treat you differently?"

I shake my head. "My father loved my mother. It was so obvious. He was fierce and loyal. When I was little, I dreamed of marrying a man like him."

"You don't want a fierce and loyal husband?"

"I do but when she died, when he realized he couldn't protect her from a disease, it changed him."

"Can you blame him, *królewna*?"

It's not hard to imagine how they must have felt about each other because there is a crackle of that same emotion between me and Aleksy. I have no doubt in my mind that once Aleksy and I are married, he will burn the world down around us to keep me safe. He's done it once, and if provoked, he'd do it again.

"Why do you want me? My father and brothers call you 'the Monk' because you're never seen with a woman. Why did you ask my father to marry me?"

"Do you want the truth?"

"Of course."

He unfolds his long body and stands to his full height. I'm completely mesmerized by the way he moves. His body is all lean muscle straining against his dark button-down shirt and black pants. He unbuttons his shirt, revealing the hard planes of his chest. "Scoot over," he demands, lifting the covers.

"What are you doing?" Being near him in such an intimate way makes me nervous. Maybe it's my own inexperience or maybe it's the way he makes me feel whenever he looks at me, like I'm the only other person in the world beside him.

"Isn't it obvious?" He moves to climb into bed beside me, forcing me to scoot toward the opposite side. "This is my bed, and I want to lay in it."

I keep the edge of the duvet clutched in my hand, watching, and waiting for him to move. When he doesn't immediately reach for me, I relax. "You didn't answer my question. Why do you want me?"

"It's simple. Business. Marrying you is the quickest and easiest way to align the Zajaks with your family."

My heart falls. His answer shouldn't surprise me, but it does. We hardly know each other and what he says makes complete sense, but it doesn't stop the truth from stinging.

"Lucia." The gentle yet commanding way he says my name draws my attention. "Come here."

I inch closer toward him but when it's not enough, he wraps a hand around my waist and drags me the rest of the way, closing the distance between us.

"It's not business anymore."

My voice shakes as I ask, "What is it, then?"

The hand on my waist slithers over my hip, down my thigh and nestles between my legs. "When I saw you for the first time, it was like an avalanche hit me. You were beautiful, sure, but you were still fighting when it seemed like the other girls gave up. That's the kind of woman I want."

A nervous laugh escapes my lips. "It was all a front. I was terrified."

"Fuck, I'm trying to keep my hands to myself, but you make it so hard." He groans as his hand slips away. I latch on to it, keeping it in place. His eyes, normally a pale icy blue, darken. "I will not force you, *jedyna moja.*"

"What does that mean," I whisper.

"I'll tell you on our wedding day."

I lean forward to brush a teasing kiss across his lips. "Tell me now."

"*Jedyna moja,*" he repeats. "My only one."

With my hand still holding his against me, I press myself against it. Electricity surges through me at the exquisite pressure his touch creates. When he calls me *królewna,* butterflies spring to life inside my belly but hearing him call me his only one? I want it to be true.

"I want this," I whisper, pressing my face against his chest. "I want you. Please, Aleksy."

"Do you know what you're asking me?" His words are a growl against my skin as he rolls me onto my back and covers me with his body. His hardness is pressed against me, telling me he wants the same thing. "Once I start, once I have you, I'm never going to stop. You'll be mine completely. You think I'm protective now? After tonight, you'll never leave my bed again."

He kisses me; it's the kind of kiss that consumes and claims. He demands I open for him, swiping his tongue along the seam of my lips until they part. And then he wrenches himself away with a snarl. "Fuck! I don't have protection."

I blink, caught off guard. "What?"

"They call me 'The Monk,' baby. I haven't touched a woman in years. I'm not prepared for this."

"Oh. I am." His eyebrows pop up and I giggle. "I've been on birth control for years."

"*Kocham çie,*" he mutters before slipping his hands under my T-shirt.

"What does that mean?"

"For now? It means my eternal gratitude but when I'm ready, I'll tell you what it really means."

# NINE

## ALEKSY

"COME CLOSER, *królewna*. I want to touch you." I sit on the edge of the bed waiting for her to shuffle toward me. Her hips sway as she moves forward and there's a shy smile on her lips. My reaction to seeing her is giving her the confidence to own her sexiness. When she's in front of me, I reach up and tug on her pale pink nipples. They stiffen under my touch, begging for more attention which I'm all too happy to give. I cup one of her full breasts in my hand and lean forward, swiping my tongue over the firm peak.

"Your tits are gorgeous." This is what makes Lucia blush. Not that I asked her to strip but commenting on her body embarrasses her. She places a hand across her chest and turns away from me. "Don't look away, Lucia. I want to see all of you."

Her body is soft and supple with curves made for my hands. She turns her head to face me but her gaze remains averted. "Drop your hands. Don't cover yourself for me. Ever."

When she does and I can finally see all of her, I exhale. She's the most gorgeous woman I've seen.

My cock is hard and eager, waiting for its turn, but it'll have to be patient. Lucia is a virgin and without proper preparation, this will be a less than pleasurable experience for us both.

"You can tell me to stop at any time," I say. "If I do something you don't like, tell me. I want you to feel good, Lucia. Do you understand."

"Yes," she breathes out when I latch on to her breast and suck her nipple between my teeth before releasing it with a pop.

"Good girl."

Dirty thoughts race through my mind. All the ways I want to defile her, taste her, use her, pleasure her. I remind myself to go slow, to be careful. God knows what she witnessed while the Nowaks held her captive, and I don't want to ruin this experience by triggering those memories.

I slip a tentative finger between her folds, which elicits a gasp from her beautiful lips. She's wet but far from ready. I tease her with one finger before adding a second, deliberately stroking her until she starts to pant and places her hands on my shoulders.

"Can I taste you, Lucia?" I look up for her approval. Having her bare pussy in front of me makes me insane with desire. I need to taste her. I lift my fingers to my lips and suck her juices from them but it's not enough.

She answers by pressing a knee to the edge of the bed. "Take what you want, *il mio re*."

I wrap my arms around her, and we tumble backward. Then I pull her up until she's straddling me, giving me the perfect view of her pussy. I groan in anticipation of the first swipe of my tongue along her folds.

"Are you ready, *moja kochana*," I ask before placing a kiss inside her thigh. Her sweet scent hits my nose, and I can't control my need to taste her. I keep her steady as I feast, dragging my tongue through her seam. She tastes heavenly, like honey. My tongue glides along her folds, lapping up her juices. I nibble on her clit, sucking it between my teeth, teasing it with my tongue until small moans escape her lips.

"Aleksy," she breathes out.

"Tell me," I coax. "Tell me what I do to you, baby."

"I'm on fire. All of me," she gasps when I slide a finger inside her and begin pumping. "It's too much. I'm going to burst."

I take pride in being the first man to make her come, to be the first to touch her, to be the first inside her. If I have my way, I'll be the only man she'll ever know or ever want.

"Aleksy, *please*."

"Come all over my face, baby," I purr as I rapidly pump my finger in and out of her until she explodes, flooding me with her orgasm. Her body shivers and shakes over me while I drink every drop of her release. Slowly, the tension in her body releases and she sags against me, resting her head against my chest.

"Are you all right," I ask, tracing lazy circles on her back.

"*Mmm*," she hums.

"Do you want more?" Her head pops up and there is a hint of trepidation in her gaze. "I was simply asking if you're ready for my cock inside you." I lift my hips, pressing myself between her legs, letting her feel how much I want her. When she doesn't respond, I roll us both until she's flat on her back. "I need an answer, *królewna*. Are you ready for my cock inside you?"

She places her hand on my check; her thumb grazes my bottom lip before she drags it all the way down to my hip.

She seems hesitant to continue, her gaze asking for permission to touch me. I cover her hand with my own and guide it to my hard length.

"Touch me," I whisper. The hesitant caress of her fingers along the ridges of my cock makes me hiss. It's torture to let her continue but I do it because I want her to feel comfortable with me. I want her to learn to express her needs and desires.

"Do you want me to use my mouth on you?"

"I don't expect anything in return. Tonight is only about doing what makes you comfortable."

"Thank you," she says with a sweet smile and a sigh.

"When you're ready for more, tell me. For now, your touch is all I need."

She continues to explore me with her hand, stroking my entire length, brushing her thumb along the tip before I hear her whisper, "I'm ready."

"I'll go slow," I tell her as my hand grazes the length of her body and dips between her thighs. I press two fingers inside her, pumping them a few times in and out, preparing her to take my length. "Spread your legs, baby."

It takes all my self-control not to surge inside her and fuck her wildly once the head of my cock is notched against her entrance, but I remind myself over and over to take my time. Once I'm rooted inside her, I stop. "Are you okay?"

She nods but I can sense her discomfort. "I'm fine."

I pull back slightly before thrusting back into her. She groans but doesn't ask me to stop. I test her boundaries, pulling out all the way before pumping deep into her.

"Talk to me, baby," I pant. "Tell me what you need."

Her mouth opens and then quickly closes. "I don't know," she finally tells me.

I smile at the thought of teaching her the language of wanton desire. "Then tell me what you want."

"Kiss me," she begs.

She lifts her face in anticipation but instead, I press my lips to her neck, sucking on the delicate skin before swiping my tongue over the fresh red bloom. With every thrust into her, it's hard to remain in control. The way she feels with my dick sheathed deep inside her pussy is heavenly.

"More," she demands.

"Are you sure?"

She nods her head. "Do your worst."

My arms slip around her body, pulling her up so she straddles me. I drive up into her over and over as she digs her nails into my shoulders. The sting of pain is delicious; it reminds me of what I'm doing to her. Owning her. Claiming her.

Like all good things, fucking her comes to an end. She feels too good and it's hard for me to make this last. Mentally, I promise us both to do better next time. She's going to learn so much and I'm going to enjoy teaching her all the ways I can please her. Next time, I'm going to make her scream, and then I'll make her beg for mercy.

With a final thrust, I explode into her, roaring through my own orgasm. I cling to her, riding out wave after wave of aftershocks.

I hear her sigh and I laugh. We're not done. Her pussy is still filled with my semi-hard cock, and I'll be damned if she's left unsatisfied. I sneak a hand between our bodies and press it against her clit, circling it with my fingers until she starts to moan.

"Give me another one, *królewna*," I coax her as she grinds her hips against me. "Come for me again."

Her entire body tenses and her mouth falls open, a

silent scream escaping before she groans, her entire body shuddering with release. She collapses against me, our sweat-slicked skin hot and sticky. I run my hand through her hair, pulling it off her neck and kissing her bare shoulder.

"Watching you come undone is the most gorgeous thing I've ever seen, *moja kochana*," I whisper against her skin between fluttering kisses along her jaw and cheek.

"What does that mean?"

"My love."

# TEN

## LUCIA

FOR DAYS, we remain secluded inside Aleksy's house, watching and waiting for signs the Nowaks are still alive and preparing to strike. During the day, Aleksy barricades himself in his office with his brother Jakub, searching for them and poring over intelligence gathered off the streets like two Army generals preparing for battle. At night, Aleksy is my teacher, showing me how much pleasure he can extract from my body.

Tonight, it's just me. He's been locked away in his office with Jakub. This is the part of being in the mafia I hate—the secrets, especially when his business involves both of our lives.

I take a long shower, luxuriating in the hot water as it hits my sore body. It no longer bears the marks of the Nowaks, but instead, shows evidence of Aleksy's passion. The only lingering reminder of my ordeal is the yellowing bruise fading near my eye.

When I step out of the shower, Aleksy is there, waiting for me, a hungry look in his eyes.

He stalks his way forward, closing in on me quickly

despite the size of the master bathroom. He reaches out and grabs a towel, holding it out for me with a smirk. "I've missed you."

"I've been here the whole time," I remind him. "I can't leave, remember?"

"I'm aware of where you were the entire day. It doesn't mean I didn't miss you." He lifts his hand and presses his thumb down on my bottom lip. "I've been fantasizing about your mouth and how it might feel wrapped around my cock. Will you get down on your knees for me, *królewna?*"

How do I tell him it's the one thing I won't do? That him even suggesting it makes me nauseous. I want to please him, to give him what he wants, but getting on my knees to suck his cock?

"Lucia." His voice shakes me from my thoughts. "You don't have to."

His brow his furrowed and the corners of his mouth are turned down into a concerned frown.

"The Nowaks . . ." I don't bother finishing the rest of my thought. Instead, I brush past Aleksy, hurrying into the bedroom to hopefully avoid this conversation.

"You haven't told me what Tytus Nowak did."

I stop in the middle of the room. "He made me watch."

"I'm sorry, *moja kochana.*"

"It's fine," I say, doing my best to move on from the conversation. "I'm tired tonight. Can we just . . . sleep?"

"Of course." He slips his hand into his pocket and pulls something out. "I have something to give you first."

He holds his hand out, revealing a black velvet ring box in the center of his palm. "What's that?"

"Your engagement ring. Jakub and I spent the morning looking for it in my office." The ring box opens with a creak, revealing a round-cut diamond flanked by two round sapphires. "It was my mother's."

"Aleksy, I can't take your mother's ring."

"Why not?" There's confusion in his gaze, and maybe the burn of anger too.

"Our marriage is arranged. Why would you want to give something so precious to someone you don't even love?"

"This ring belongs to my future wife. That's you. You're the only wife I plan to have."

"Then give it to Jakub."

He snaps the box closed and steps toward me. "Why are you so scared of this ring?"

It's not the ring I'm scared of, it's the feelings I'm starting to develop. I learned early on when it comes to the mafia, love is a losing game. If you love someone, they can be taken from you, used as a weapon, or worse, used to betray you. I don't want to let myself fall in love with Aleksy because I couldn't bear the thought of losing him.

"*Kocham çie*," he says softly as he shuffles back to the bed and sits down on the edge. He looks up at me, and the wounded look on his face guts me.

"Are you going to tell me what that means?"

"It means 'I love you,' Lucia."

A gasp escapes my lips. "You don't mean that."

He nods. "Yes, I do. I love you, Lucia."

"How is that even possible?" Love is supposed to take time to develop, right?

"It's possible," he says with a sigh. "I'm inexplicably in love with you."

A buzzing sound breaks the tension between us. He reaches into his pocket, pulls out his phone, and answers.

There's a brief, tense exchange in Polish before he pushes to his feet.

"I have to go," he says.

"Where?" My heartbeat increases, thundering rapidly in my chest. This isn't the plan. We're supposed to stay put and wait. It's why he sent Jakub out in the streets to search for signs of the Nowaks.

"You know I can't tell you."

"When will you be back?"

He shrugs. "In a few hours? I don't know."

"This doesn't feel right," I say, panic filling my voice. "I don't think you should go."

"Well, *królewna*, I'm sorry but I run this family, not you. When duty calls, I must answer."

"What about your duty to protect me? You promised you wouldn't leave me alone."

"You won't be alone. My men are here patrolling. If anything happens, they'll keep you safe."

My panic morphs into desperation as the pit in my stomach grows heavier, leaving me no choice but to use my body as a weapon. My fingers twist the knot in the towel above my breasts, loosening it until the towel falls to the floor.

"What are you doing, *królewna*?"

"Whatever it takes to make sure you stay," I tell him as I advance toward him with measured steps. He watches me, his gaze traveling the length of my body. His entire body is wound tight with tension.

"I didn't think manipulation was your game." His voice is cold. When I stop in front of him, he turns his head to the side. My hands reach out, grasping his belt, but his cover mine, gripping them tight. "Lucia, if you do this—"

"You'll stop loving me?"

"No." His voice is rough and heavy. He faces me, and the look in his eye is like a punch to the gut. He's not furious; he's hurt. A single tear slips down his cheek. "Is this the woman you truly are? Willing to use my love as a weapon against me?"

I step back ashamed and disgusted. Love isn't something you exploit but I tried to do it. Maybe I already did.

"When I get back, we'll discuss this," he says sharply before brushing past me to leave.

An image of my mother kissing my father good-bye floods my thoughts. Whenever he left, she always kissed him and told him she loved him. She told me it was in case he didn't come back.

"I always want your father to know he's loved," she said.

If Aleksy doesn't come back, I want him to know the same thing. I search for my discarded clothing and tug the t-shirt over my head. It's enough to cover me without being too indecent before rushing toward the door. "Wait," I call after him. "Aleksy, wait!"

He hits the bottom of the stairs and looks up. "I have to go, Lucia. Whatever game you want to play now, save it."

I dash down the stairs, my hand ghosting over the railing and when I nearly trip, he hurries up to catch me. "Christ, *królewna*, whatever it is you need to say isn't worth breaking your neck."

"Yes, it is," I insist. I throw my arms around his neck, hugging him tight, inhaling his now familiar fresh scent. He seems reluctant to return my affection but soon, his arms slip around me with their comfortable warmth and weight. "I love you," I whisper.

"Don't say it if you don't mean it."

I pull back a bit to look him in the eye. His handsomeness is breathtaking, especially when he's dressed to kill in an all-black suit. "I mean it. I love you."

He reaches up, cupping my face with his hands and kisses me tenderly. "If I die tonight, then I'll die a happy man."

"Don't say that! Promise to come home, Aleksy."

His glacial blue eyes trap me in their gaze. "Nothing could stop me from returning to you, *moja kochana*."

# ELEVEN

## ALEKSY

LUCIA'S LOVE is like wearing a bulletproof vest. It's an added layer of armor, protecting me against whatever might happen tonight.

When Jakub arrives, he asks me about Lucia. "She doesn't like that I'm gone," I say. I'm not entirely certain I like being gone, either.

"The sooner these assholes show, the quicker you can stick your dick back—"

"Watch what you say, brother. At the end of the week, Lucia will be my wife."

Shadowy figures emerge from the dark and head in our direction. Jakub moves closer to me, prepared to strike if necessary. But I know neither of us will be using our weapons tonight.

Lucia's brothers, Nero and Anthony, stop a few feet away. "Gentleman," Nero says with a nod. "Thank you for meeting us."

"I don't appreciate being called away when I'm in the middle of planning my wedding," I state.

Nero sneers. "I heard about the deal you made with my

father. You get Lucia's hand in marriage and my spot as my father's underboss."

"I'm already the head of my family. I don't want your spot, but I do want power. I saw an opportunity and I took it. Can you blame me?"

"No, I don't, but you'll never become my father's underboss."

I roll my neck from side-to-side and sigh. I've been playing games like this for years. I make a deal with one person and someone else comes along thinking they can put an end to it. It never works out for the other guy.

"Are you going to stop me?" My gun sits heavy against my back, tucked into the waistband of my pants, reminding me of its presence.

"No, I'm not going to take anything from you. You saved our sister; we're grateful." Nero nods toward Anthony before directing his attention back to me. "But you'd be aligning yourself with the wrong person."

"You're talking about your father."

He nods and drags a hand down his face. "I know exactly who I'm talking about. He raised me to be the man I am. He taught me how to lead my men, and unfortunately for him, he taught me how to smell a rat."

I glance toward Jakub, who looks as confused as I feel. "What are you talking about, Nero? Your father said someone betrayed him. That's how they got Lucia."

"I thought the same thing. I even suspected the Bianchis, but I was wrong. My father let the wolves into the hen house. He gave the Nowaks access to Lucia."

"Son of a bitch."

"Why would he do that," Jakub asks. "He risked his daughter's life by handing her over to Tytus and Filip."

"He thought he was sending Aleksy on a suicide

mission." Nero's gaze drifts back to me. "He thought you and Tytus would kill each other."

"And then he'd make a move into our territory."

"Precisely," Nero confirms.

For days, I've been holed up in my house with Lucia, watching and waiting for the Nowaks to show up when all along, my enemy was closer than expected. He insisted Lucia stay put with me, entrusting her with me. All for what?

"Are the Nowaks still alive?" I needed to figure out who the real threat was before I made my next move.

Nero shakes his head. "My men found them last night. Filip and Tytus are resting comfortably at the bottom of the Cuyahoga. They won't turn up for a while."

"And your father? What are you going to do about him?"

He sticks his hands in his pockets and rocks back on his heels. "That's why I called this meeting. You were promised something, and once my bastard of a father is dead, I'll be head of the Giordanos. You kept your end of the bargain by saving my sister. Why shouldn't I keep his end of the bargain?"

"I'm marrying Lucia," I state.

"If that's all you want, then we're done here. But I thought you wanted power."

I take a step closer to him. "What are you proposing?"

He smiles and chuckles. The sound is sinister, giving me second thoughts. What if none of this is true? I'm accepting his information without a single piece of evidence.

"You're smart. I'm brutal. Let's join forces. Once you marry Lucia, you'll be family anyway. No more Zajaks, no more Giordanos. Just family."

"No more Zajaks," I mumble.

My father worked to make us powerful, to make our name not only known but feared and respected. But it was his work, not mine. When he died, I inherited what he created. Nero's offer could be the perfect opportunity to set myself apart from my father's legacy.

"I'm tempted but I need proof. I'm not going to be used as a pawn in whatever sick game you might be playing with your father. And if your sister is somehow involved . . ."

I didn't want to think Lucia could be capable of such a disgusting level of duplicity.

"She's not involved in anything," Nero insists, "and I'm telling the truth. But I don't blame you for wanting evidence. Being suspicious is smart."

He turns to Anthony, who pulls a phone from a pocket inside his jacket and hands it to me. I swipe to unlock the screen and play the video already cued up. Massimo Giordano is on the screen sitting in the back of his chauffeured town car. He's on the phone talking with someone and only his side of the conversation is audible.

"I just left Zajak's estate," he says. "I convinced him and Lucia to stay put. I don't know how long he's going to last so you better figure something out. If you're lucky, my daughter will spread her legs for the bastard, and you'll have more time to plan."

What plan is he talking about and to whom is he talking?

"Tytus, if you show up at his house, he's going to shoot you in the head."

I end the video. I don't need or want to watch anymore. It's clear Massimo is working with the Nowaks, perhaps to finally make his way into Cleveland. What troubles me the most is Lucia being left alone.

"Jakub," I call out. "Call the men patrolling the house. Make sure everything's okay."

After a few minutes, my brother looks up from his phone and shrugs. "No one is answering. I don't know what's going on."

"I do," I hiss. "Massimo is making his move."

# TWELVE

## LUCIA

THE FEELING of impending doom doesn't relent. Nothing I do to relax brings me relief, so I spend most of the evening pacing the family room. It has a massive picture window revealing a breathtaking view of the lake. Tonight, the moon glistens off the turbulent waves crashing against the shoreline.

The doorbell ringing makes me jump but before I can answer, one of Aleksy's men intercepts me.

"Wait here," he says before consulting the tiny screen of his phone. "Do you know him?"

I sigh and nod. "It's my father. You can let him in."

Perhaps Aleksy asked him to come over and help keep me safe from the Nowaks. When the door opens and my father appears, I rush forward to embrace him but stop in my tracks at the sight of the gun pointed in my direction.

"What are you doing," I gasp.

Instead of answering my question, he shoots my temporary guard before turning the gun back toward me. "Where's Aleksy," he snaps.

"He's not here." Hot tears sting my eyes. "What's going on? Why did you just kill someone?"

I glance down at the man's body. Blood seeps from his wound, spreading around him and seeping onto the fabric of my new silk robe.

My father steps forward, grabs me by the arm and drags me back into the family room. "Sit down." He tosses me onto the plush cream sofa. "Where did he go?"

"I don't know." It's hard to concentrate when my father has a gun in my face, "He got a phone call earlier and left."

"And he just left you here? Alone?" The sinister tone of my father's voice makes me shiver.

"What's going on, Dad?"

"Don't call me that," he says through clenched teeth. "I'm not your father, Lucia."

"What?" I repeat.

"It's simple to understand, Lucia. Your mother fucked someone else, got pregnant, and tried to pass you off as mine."

"But she loved you!" Images from my childhood flash through my mind. They seemed happy and in love. "And you loved her, didn't you?"

"Of course I loved your mother. That's why her betrayal was like a knife to the chest. She would have never told me if she didn't get sick, but apparently, her death bed was the perfect time to tell me she'd been unfaithful."

"You've known this entire time?" The change in my father after my mother's death makes perfect sense now. It wasn't her death that hardened him and made him distant; it was her betrayal.

"Now you know why I let that fucking Polack have you. I'd never let my real daughter marry a piece of trash like Aleksy Zajak."

"Then why did you send him after me? Why not let the Nowaks kill me?"

He laughs. "Sweetheart, I let the Nowaks take you and I sent him after you hoping they'd kill you both, but these assholes are like cockroaches. Nothing kills them. I hate having to do everything myself."

"So, you're going to kill me yourself?" Tears stream down my cheeks. "How can you do this to me? I love you."

"I wish I could say the same, Lucia."

Movement from behind my father catches my eyes but I've been taught well enough not make a scene. As Aleksy creeps into the room, his gun pointed at the back of my father's head, a finger to his lips, my heart rate increases.

"How can you punish me for something I didn't do? Do you even know who my real father is?"

"Of course I do. Your father's Lou Gambino, but he's dead too. You'll be joining him soon enough."

Aleksy makes his move, striding forward. "Not if I have anything to say about it."

My father smirks. "How kind of you to join us, Aleksy. You're in quite the predicament because if you shoot me, I won't hesitate to use my last breath to kill Lucia."

"That's not going to happen." Nero enters the room behind Aleksy and positions himself on the side of my father. "There are two guns pointed straight at you, old man. Drop the weapon or one of us shoots."

My father bends, placing his gun on the floor, before standing back up. "Never thought you were the type to betray me, Nero."

"Never thought you'd be willing to kill your own daughter," Nero replies.

"She's not my daughter!" His outburst makes me flinch. "She's nothing to me."

His cruelty breaks my heart as dreams of having him give me away on my wedding day dissolve. All I want to do is disappear into the fabric of the couch.

"Lucia." My gaze travels to Aleksy. "Go upstairs. I don't want you to watch what happens next."

"Are you going to kill him?"

"If you asked me to spare his life, I would," he says before glancing over at my brother. "But I'm not so sure about Nero."

"Enemies need to be punished," Nero reminds me.

"He's your father. You make the call." I stand up and give one last impassive look at the man I thought was my father. My chest aches because it feels like my entire life was a lie. I can't tell fact from fiction.

I take each step one-by-one back upstairs to the master bedroom and wait. I notice the blood on the hem of my robe, so I take it into the bathroom and try to get it out. It's just a distraction because every few minutes, I stop and listen, anticipating the sound of a gunshot. When it doesn't happen, I carry on until the robe is spotless.

What are they waiting for? I don't want him to die but I know he wasn't going to show me the same mercy. The man I thought was my father, Massimo Giordano, was planning to kill me without an ounce of remorse. Does that mean he deserves the same brutality? He would say yes.

"Letting your enemy live is a sign of weakness," he once told me. "If you find one good thing to justify your leniency, then you'll keep looking for it in all of your enemies until it backfires."

When it finally happens, the sound of the gun shots catches me off guard. I lulled myself into a false sense of security, choosing to believe Aleksy and Nero wouldn't follow through with killing Massimo. But they're cut from the same cloth; enemies are punished, justice is swift.

It seems like hours before Aleksy comes upstairs. He opens the door and stands in the threshold, watching me and waiting.

"It's done," he says.

"I know," I tell him with a sniffle. "I heard."

He strides forward and perches in front of me. There are flecks of red on his cheek. I reach up and rub them with the pad of my thumb until they're gone.

"No one will hurt you again, *moja kochana*," he says, turning his face toward my hand. He clutches it to his cheek and kisses my palm.

I lean forward to kiss him, pressing my lips against his with a hard, demanding kiss. He opens for me but swiftly takes over, sliding his tongue against mine. Our teeth clash as I fight for the control he took, until I grow frustrated and tug him toward me. I want all of him, every inch, to cover me. I want him to consume me and swallow me whole because tonight has been a night too full of revelations. Love and loss together. And right now, I need to be loved.

My hands slide over his shoulders and claw at his back, pulling up his shirt until he pushes me away and works to unbutton his shirt. My hands slide under the waistband of my panties, and I begin to slide them off until Aleksy stops me.

"Are you sure you want to do this? I don't want to be the asshole and take advantage of you," he says.

"It's the only thing I want," I breathe out. "I need to know that the love between us is real."

He grips the lace fabric of my panties in his fist and tugs, ripping them away from my body. "It's the realest fucking thing I've ever felt."

The moment he surges inside me, I feel whole, complete. His hands grip my waist, his fingers dig into my skin as he watches his cock glide in and out of me. Groans and growls escape his lips; he sounds like a wild beast, but when he looks up at me, there is nothing but love and adoration in his gaze. Only then does he slow down to lean forward and brush a kiss across my lips.

"Today, you become my queen," he pants. "*Królowa.*"

# THIRTEEN

## ALEKSY

"DO you still want to get married on Friday?" Lucia stretches out her delicious body next to me and it's tempting to reach out, pull her on top of me and fuck her again. But I like to think I'm a man who has self-control.

"You don't?" I pin her to the mattress and place a lazy, lingering kiss on her lips.

Her smile is shy. "We can wait now, can't we? There isn't a rush since my father... I mean, Massimo is dead. And so are the Nowaks."

"We could wait, but why do you want to? Unless you're having second thoughts?"

"No, I'm not," she insists. "But don't you want a proper wedding?"

"You mean in the church with hundreds of guests we barely know? Spending thousands of dollars on a party we don't even get to enjoy?"

"Well, when you put it like that..."

"Lucia, if it's truly what you want, then I'll do it. I'll do anything for you."

She snuggles into me, sliding an arm around my neck,

pressing herself against me. "I'll think about it," she says with a sigh. Minutes later, her body is relaxed, and her breaths are soft and even.

It feels wrong to be so happy after Massimo's death. I didn't pull the trigger, but I watched as his son did. There wasn't an ounce of remorse on Nero's face, and I regretted making a deal with him. Only someone without a soul could murder their own father and not feel guilt. Lucia hasn't asked about Massimo's death, or about her brother, but one day she will, and I hope to give her the answers she seeks.

For now, we both have to be content with the fact the immediate danger presented by both the Nowaks and Massimo Giordano is gone. Living a life in the shadows, a life less than honorable according to society's standards, will always be a risk but it's one I'm comfortable living if she's waiting for me at the end of the day.

Eventually, I manage a few hours of sleep and when I wake up, she's gone. Her side of the bed is still warm, so I know she hasn't been awake for long, so I get dressed and go hunting. Luckily for me, she's in the kitchen working hard at making a huge mess.

"What are you doing, *królowa*?" I ask with a laugh as I walk toward her.

She turns to me, her face streaked with flour, and frowns. "I liked when you called me *królewna* better."

"I'll call you whatever you want as long as you tell me what on earth you're doing."

"Trying to make pierogi." She looks at the ingredients spread out in front of her. "It's just like ravioli, right? Same kind of dough, only bigger?"

I roll my eyes and groan. "Lucia! They are not the same thing."

"Then teach me how to make them."

"I can't," I admit. I walk over to the refrigerator and open the freezer door. "I buy them all pre-made from the West Side Market."

"Then come and figure it out with me," she demands, holding up a bag of flour.

"I would love to, but I have to bury a body."

Her face and the bag of flour falls. "Shit!" She looks down at the mess and instantly bursts into tears. "I'm sorry. I'll clean it up."

I rush toward her and take her into my arms. "I'm an asshole. I should have been more considerate of your feelings."

"It's fine," she says with a sniffle.

"No, it's not." I gather her into my arms and stroke her hair. "Come with me. Nero said he was going to call the cemetery where your mother is buried and have Massimo put there."

"I don't want him anywhere near my mother," she growls.

"You can tell that to your brother then. I'm sure he will respect your wishes." I help her stand and brush the flour from her t-shirt. "You don't have to go."

"I want to make sure he's dead and can't come back to hurt you or me."

"He is dead, *moja kochana*," I insist. "You wiped his blood from my face last night."

"I'm still going to come with you."

I nod my head before taking her back upstairs to get ready for the day. The mess in the kitchen will be cleaned up by the time we return; I have people to take care of it for me. An hour later, Lucia emerges from the bedroom dressed in a pair of jeans and a cream-colored sweater. Her dark hair is braided to the side and her face is bare, with nothing but a few freckles sprinkled across her skin. Her beauty is breathtaking and once again, I remind myself of my good fortune.

She's silent as we drive more than hour from Cleveland to Youngstown. There are moments when I want to ask her what she is thinking or even feeling but when I was in her position, I wanted to be left alone. When she's ready to talk, I'll be here to listen.

Nero is waiting in his shiny black Mercedes at the front of the entrance. I pull next to him and get out, warning Lucia to stay put until I talk to him.

"Is everything arranged?"

He nods. "All it took was a sizable donation to the church," he says.

"Your sister doesn't want Massimo buried with your mother."

"The church still maintains a pauper's section. He will be buried there with a simple marker."

"Thank you." We both turn to find Lucia standing near the back of the car.

"I would have tossed him in the Mahoning River if you asked," he says as he approaches her slowly. "I am sorry this happened."

She accepts his embrace and his comfort. It's odd watching him console Lucia after witnessing the ruthless way he murdered his father last night.

With his arm still around Lucia, Nero turns to me. "You're going to take care of her, right? My father had no right to give her away, but I won't take her from you if I know you're going to protect her."

"Lucia is mine," I tell him. "Even if you tried to take her from me, I'd move heaven and earth to get her back and you'd likely end up dead."

"Do you want my permission or not?"

I shake my head. "We're getting married on Friday with or without it." I glance toward Lucia who's gnawing on her bottom lip. "But it would mean the world to your sister, and to me, if you gave us your blessing."

I would do anything for her, including capitulating to her brother, if it meant making her smile. She looks over to her brother with big, pleading eyes and when he relents, her face transforms.

"Thank you, Nero," she says, adding a kiss to his cheek.

"I get to walk you down the aisle," he says gruffly.

# FOURTEEN

## LUCIA

"I'M PRETTY SURE this is bad luck," I pant as Aleksy fills me with his cock.

"I don't give a shit," he groans, thrusting deep into me. "Fuck, Lucia!"

He presses his hand flat against my back, pushing my body into the mattress as I grasp for the covers with my hands, clawing at them until I give in and succumb to the demands of Aleksy's body.

"You're going to walk down the aisle dripping," he moans, slapping his hand across the bare skin of my ass. "I want your brother to smell the sex on you."

"Aleksy," I gasp.

"Just a bit longer, baby. I promise not to make you too sore for our wedding day."

He soothes a hand down my band, stroking his fingers along my waist. I love the way he touches me with such reverence. It makes me believe in the power of our connection. It's been a little more than a week since he rescued me from the depravity of the Nowaks, and yet, it feels like a lifetime. Love is incomprehensible. I reach behind me for one of the hands digging into my hips and grab it, pulling it and him forward.

"Alesky," I breathe out his name as his lips brush against my shoulder. "I love you."

"I love you too, *królewna*. So much." He places a hand behind my knee and lifts it to the mattress, deepening our connection, forcing a moan from my lips. This new angle hits every spot, igniting a furious blaze inside me.

Sweat prickles along my brow line and my body tenses, ready to be pushed into my impending climax. He pulls out all the way to the tip before slamming into me, sending me straight into bliss. I cry out as he squeezes my hips and roars through his own release. His entire body stills, all I feel is the pulsing of his cock against my walls.

He holds me through the aftershocks, trailing kisses along the ridge of my shoulder, brushing his fingers along my rib cage before settling his hand over my belly. "I never wanted children," he whispers. "I didn't want to bring an innocent child into this life, but you've made me reconsider my future."

Children. I never thought about being a mother either. I'm young and while I loved my mother, being raised amongst criminals was not the happiest part of my childhood. Massimo moved us all out to a farm in Canfield to escape, but trouble always founds us.

"You're awfully quiet," Aleksy murmurs. "Do you not want to have children, Lucia?"

I don't know how to answer him. "You said something to me a few day ago, and said you'd tell me what it meant on our wedding day."

"*Sprawiasz, że chcę być lepszym człowiekiem.*"

"That's it. Tell me what it means."

"You make me want to be a better person."

I turn my head slightly to glance at him. "Do you mean that? Do you want to be better?"

"I'm willing to do whatever it takes to be worthy of your love."

What more could I ask him for? He's already proven capable of protecting me and I'd never ask him to give up his position of power in the Cleveland underworld. He is a made man; the mob is his life. Men try to escape this criminal world of darkness, but it always sucks them back in, even against their will.

"Then there is only one thing for you to do," I tell him.

"What's that?"

"Marry me."

## THE VANISHED SERIES

Vanished In Brooklyn by Kylie Marcus

Vanished In Boston by Ava Pearl

Vanished In Chicago by ChaShiree M.

Vanished In Atlanta by Andi Lynn

Vanished In Nashville by Sammi Starlight

Vanished In Cleveland by Rebecca Gallo

Vanished In Manhattan by Matilda Martel

Vanished In Denver by Layne Daniels

Vanished In Baltimore by Alana Winters

Vanished In Vegas by S.E Isaac

Vanished In Newark by M.K Moore

# ALSO BY REBECCA GALLO

The Presidential Promises Duet:

Presidential Bargain

Capitol Promises

Heart Campaign

The Ripley Trilogy:

Ceremony of Lust

Flirt Club Collaborations:

Resolution Wanderlust

Dear Mr. Temporary

Forever True

Mr. Cream

His Cactus Flower

Wanderlust Wedding

Her Yankee Doodle Daddy

Cowboy's Melody

Forget Me Knot

Just Perfect: A Flirt Club Collection

Other Collaborations

Academic Integrity (Scandalous Daddies Club Book 1)

Academic Dishonesty (Scandalous Daddies Club Book 2)

Mature Content (Scandalous Daddies Club Book 3)

Parental Discretion (Scandalous Daddies Club Book 4)

Daddy in Disguise (Halloween Steam)

Royally Scrooged (The Holiday Honeys)

# ABOUT THE AUTHOR

Rebecca Gallo lives in Southern Arizona with her family and a tuxedo cat, Chuck. She is a full-time high school English teacher, a taco aficionado, a doughnut connoisseur, and a wine snob.

Want to send her an email? Send it to:
authorrebeccagallo@gmail.com

Sign up for my monthly newsletter here:
https://www.subscribepage.com/y7aov3